To Angela, Caryn, and JoAnne,
and the magnanimous Gang of Four!
D. D.

For Harriet
J. M.

First edition 2004

Library of Congress Cataloging-in-Publication Data
Dodds, Dayle Ann.
Minnie's Diner / by Dayle Ann Dodds ; illustrated by John Manders. — 1st ed.
p.   cm.
Summary: Rhyming tale of five boys and their father who forget about their chores on the farm
to enjoy Minnie's good cooking, each requesting double what the previous one ordered.
ISBN 0-7636-1736-9
[1. Diners (Restaurants) — Fiction. 2. Farm life — Fiction. 3. Fathers and sons — Fiction.
4. Multiplication. 5. Stories in rhyme.] I. Manders, John, ill. II. Title.
PZ8.3.D645 Mi 2004
[E] — dc21   2002034756

2 4 6 8 10 9 7 5 3 1

Printed in China

This book was typeset in Myriad.
The illustrations were done in gouache.

Candlewick Press
2067 Massachusetts Avenue
Cambridge, Massachusetts 02140

visit us at www.candlewick.com

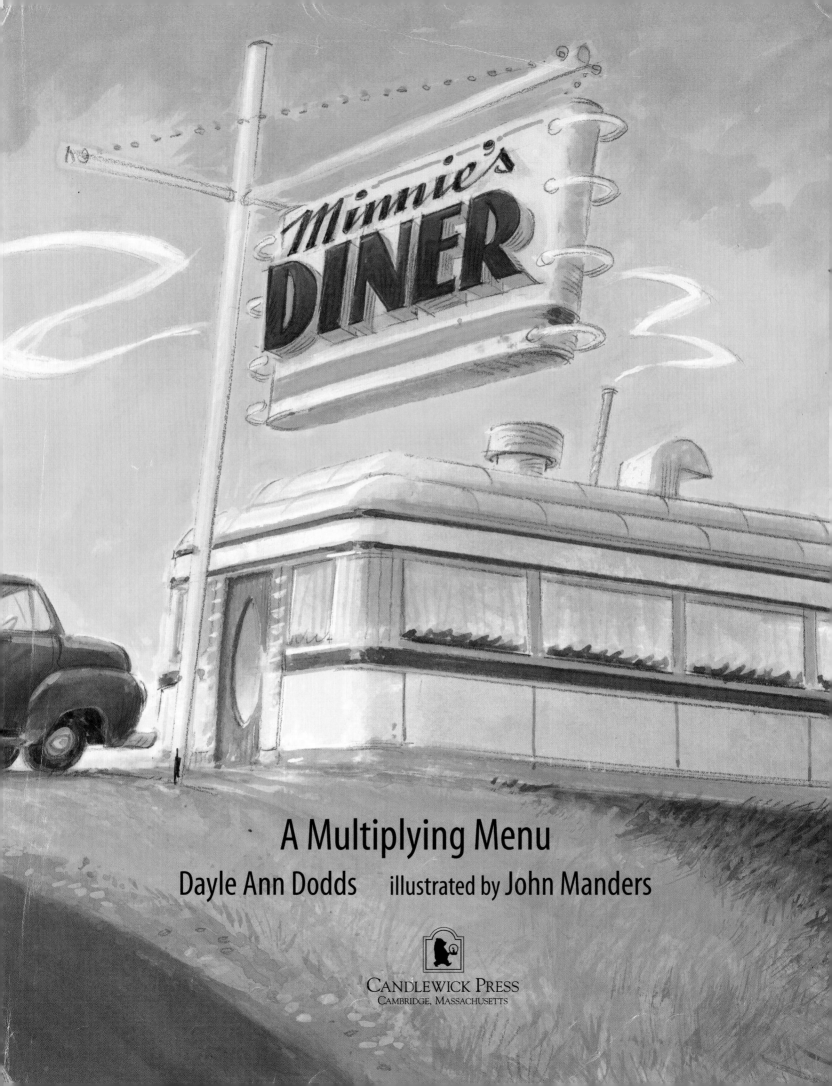

A Multiplying Menu

Dayle Ann Dodds   illustrated by John Manders

CANDLEWICK PRESS
CAMBRIDGE, MASSACHUSETTS

Across the farm, one sunny day,
bellowed the voice of Papa McFay:

"There'll be no eatin'
till your work is through.
Step lively, boys.
There's much to do!"

But Papa forgot there was nothing finer
than the scrumptious food at Minnie's Diner.

And soon, down the road from Minnie's kitchen,
wafted a smell that got the boys itchin'.

Will, the youngest, stopped milking the cow.
"I'm hungry," he said. "I need some food now!"

He raced to the diner.
He opened the door.
He took a **BIG** sniff.
He could stand it
no more!

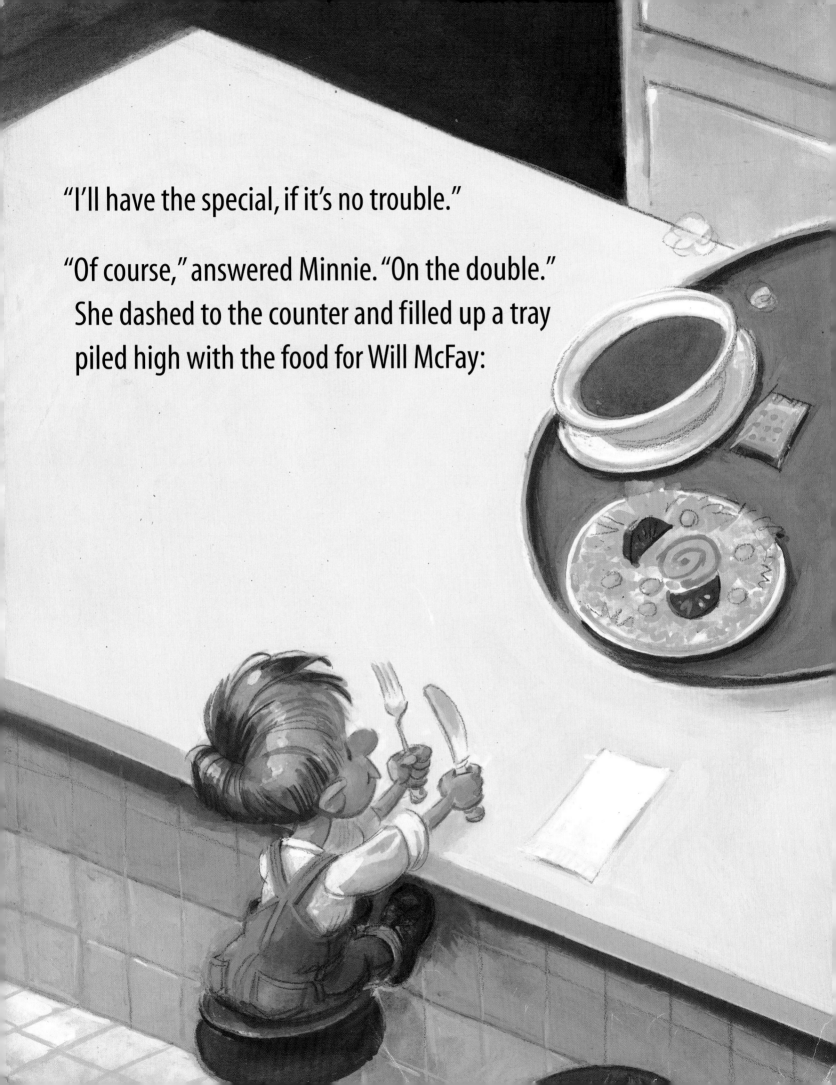

"I'll have the special, if it's no trouble."

"Of course," answered Minnie. "On the double."
She dashed to the counter and filled up a tray
piled high with the food for Will McFay:

1 soup
1 salad
1 sandwich
some fries, and
1 of her special hot cherry pies

Back on the farm,
Bill slopped the fat pig.
"I'm hungry!" said Bill,
with a jiggety-jig.

He raced to the diner.

He burst through the door,

twice as big

as his brother before.

"I'll have what Will has, but make it a double."

"Of course," said Minnie. "That's no trouble."
She dashed to the counter and filled up a tray
piled high with **2** specials for Bill McFay:

Back on the farm, Phil painted the gate.
"I'm hungry!" he said. "I just can't wait!"

He raced to the diner.

He burst through the door,

twice as big

as his brother before.

"I'll have what Bill has, but make it a double."

"Of course," said Minnie. "That's no trouble."
She dashed to the counter and filled up a tray
piled high with **4** specials for Phil McFay:

4 soups
4 salads
4 sandwiches **4** fries
and for dessert,
4 hot cherry pies

Back on the farm, Gill chopped piles of wood.
"I'm hungry," he said. "Minnie's sure would taste good!"

He raced to the diner.

He burst through the door,

twice as big

as his brother before.

"I'll have what Phil has, but make it a double."

"Of course," said Minnie. "That's no trouble.
She dashed to the counter and filled up a tray
piled high with **8** specials for Gill McFay:

Back on the farm, Dill planted the wheat.
"I'm hungry," he said, "from my head to my feet!"

He raced to the diner.

He burst through the door,

twice as big

as his brother before.

"I'll have what Gill has, but make it a double."

"Of course," said Minnie. "That's no trouble."
She dashed to the counter and filled up a tray
piled high with **16** specials for Dill McFay:

16 soups

16 salads   **16** sandwiches   **16** fries

and for dessert,
16 hot cherry pies

Back on the farm, Papa looked high and low,
up hill, down valley, and across the plateau.

The cow was not milked. The pig was not slopped.
The gate was not painted. The wood was not chopped.

"Well, wippety jiggers," said Papa McFay.
"What could have made those boys run away?"

And then, down the road from Minnie's kitchen,
wafted a smell that got Papa itchin'.

Dill just started eating,
when the floor swayed and shook.
They all turned their heads.
They all took a look.

An **ENORMOUS** shadow covered the floor, bigger than **ANY** they'd seen before.

"There'll be no eatin' till your work is through.
Step lively, boys. There's much to do!"

Papa turned to leave, but to his surprise,
his nose caught the scent of those hot cherry pies.

"Perhaps . . ." said Papa, "if it's no trouble —"

"I know," said Minnie. "Make it a

double."